Save the Reindeer!

adapted by Tone Thyne

based on the teleplay written by Chris Nee

illustrated by Michael Scanlon, Little Airplane Productions

SIMON SPOTLIGHT/NICK JR.

New York   London   Toronto   Sydney

"It's Christmas eve! Let's trim the tree," the Wonder Pets sang happily.

But while the Wonder Pets were singing,
the tin-can phone started ringing.

"It's Santa's reindeer!" shouted Tuck.
"She's on the ice, and she looks stuck."

"This is as serious as it gets,"
said Ming-Ming. "Let's go, Wonder Pets!"

They built their Christmas Flyboat fast—
first the wheels, then the mast.

They hopped aboard, and off they flew—
Linny, Tuck, and Ming-Ming, too!

They sailed on through the chilly night,
and soon the North Pole was in sight!

Linny looked high and low.
"There's the reindeer down below!"

"Look—the ice is about to break. . . .
Hurry!" said Tuck. "For Christmas's sake!"

What would our heroes use to get her?
"I know," said Ming-Ming. "Use my sweater!"

"It's teamwork time!" They gave a pull
and made a net of purple wool.

Tuck said, "Reindeer, don't be upset.
We'll save you with this purple net."

The reindeer said, "You're very nice for helping me get off the ice."

They hitched her up to Santa's sleigh and watched the reindeer fly away.

"Now let's head back home," Linny said.
"It's Christmas eve, and it's time for bed."

Through the sky the Flyboat soared,
with three holiday heroes aboard.

Back at home, the Wonder Pets found that **Christmas** cheer was all around:

presents from Santa, a star on the tree,
and best of all . . . some celery!